Veo el otoño
I See Fall

por/by Charles Ghigna

ilustrado por/illustrated by Ag Jatkowska

PICTURE WINDOW BOOKS

a capstone imprint

I see trees of red and brown.

Veo árboles rojos y marrones.

I see gold leaves on the ground.

Veo hojas doradas en el suelo.

I see apples piled high.

Veo manzanas en pilas altas.

I see buses passing by.

Veo autobuses pasar.

I see geese out on the lake.

Veo gansos en el lago.

I see waves the breezes make.

Veo las ondas que hace la brisa.

I see squirrels playing chase.

Veo ardillas jugando.

I see a jack-o'-lantern's face!

¡Veo una cara de calabaza!

I see friendly ghosts and witches.

Veo fantasmas y brujas amistosos.

I see clowns in funny britches.

Veo payasos con pantalones chistosos.

I see pumpkins on the street.

Veo calabazas en la calle.

I see friends go trick-or-treat!

¡Veo a amigos diciendo "dulce o travesura"!

I see an owl in a tree.

Veo un búho en un árbol.

I see a scarecrow wink at me.

Veo un espantapájaros que me
guiña un ojo.

I see the sun begin to set.

Veo el sol que va a caer.

I see my shadow's silhouette.

Veo la silueta de mi sombra.

I see a pink and purple sky.

Veo un cielo rosa y púrpura.

I see a homemade pumpkin pie.

Veo un pastel de calabazas casero.

I see turkey on a plate.

Veo un pavo en un plato.

I see my family celebrate.

Veo a mi familia celebrando.

The End
Fin

—for Charlotte and Christopher

Bilingual I See is published by Picture Window Books
A Capstone Imprint
1710 Roe Crest Drive
North Mankato, Minnesota 56003
www.capstonepub.com

Library of Congress Cataloging-in-Publication Data
Ghigna, Charles.
  [I see fall. Spanish & English]
  Veo el otoño = I see fall / por Charles Ghigna ; ilustrado por Ag Jatkowska.
     p. cm. — (I see)
Summary: Illustrations and easy-to-read, rhyming text show what makes autumn special,
from colorful leaves and pumpkins to Halloween and Thanksgiving festivities.
ISBN 978-1-4048-7307-0 (library binding)
1. Autumn—Juvenile fiction. 2. Stories in rhyme. [1. Stories in rhyme. 2. Autumn—Fiction.
3. Spanish language materials—Bilingual.] I. Jatkowska, Ag, ill. II. Title. III. Title: I see fall.

PZ73.G476 2012

[E]—dc23   2011048899

Original designer: Emily Harris
Bilingual adaptation designer: Danielle Ceminsky
Translation by Strictly Spanish.

Printed in the United States of America in North Mankato, Minnesota.
122012
007042R